Our Digital Lives

Cameron Macintosh

Contents

Digital Technology Today

For many of us, digital technology is like a glue that keeps us connected to one another. It allows us to make connections with people around the world and to share our interests with like-minded people. As well as helping people to keep in touch with each other, digital technology allows us to access information and communicate with the wider world in ways that would have been unimaginable to previous generations.

Online digital technology can take the form of **social media** posts, such as photos and videos, or **blogs**, which can be posted in a text or video format. We can access these types of posts through the various online **platforms** now available to us.

Smartphones allow us to access and share online content more easily.

Even with all the advantages of online technology, we still need to be mindful of problems that can arise from it. Spending time online can expose us to privacy breaches, such as **hacking**, or to **viruses** and **malware**. These threats can damage our devices or gather information about us without our permission.

Our self-esteem, or the way we feel about ourselves, can also be affected when we see how others present themselves on social media. We often only see the best parts of other people's lives and achievements online, which can make us compare our own lives or physical appearance unfavourably to theirs.

Social Media

Social media is a technology that allows people to communicate and share information through digital networks. This information can take many forms, including photos, videos or links to websites and articles.

Until the early twenty-first century, governments and private companies controlled the media that most people watched, read or listened to. They decided what people would be able to view on TV, hear on the radio or read in printed magazines and newspapers. This all changed with the arrival of social media in the late 1990s. Suddenly, people had much more control over the media they could access. People were also able to post their own content online, which they could share with anyone around the world who had access to the internet.

Username: RileyTheKing342

Interests: camping
gaming
baking
reading

Social media profiles help us to connect with others online.

Social media uses what are known as platforms: websites or **apps** where people can create profiles that others can see and interact with. Popular platforms include Instagram, Facebook, TikTok and Twitter. One of the first platforms was called “Six Degrees”. It launched in 1997 and allowed users to make their own profile to connect with friends and family, much like present-day platforms.

Social media platforms allow users to interact with each other’s profiles and posts.

Social media can be extremely useful for collaborations, such as school or work group projects, as well as for sharing interests and making connections with people we might not otherwise meet in person. It does, however, need to be used with care, as it can sometimes expose us to **misinformation**, **cyberbullying** or pressures to change the ways we look or behave that are not good for our self-esteem.

Smart Suggestions

When we read about social media, we often come across the word **algorithm**. Put simply, an algorithm is a set of digital instructions that directs a computer to do something.

Algorithms can remember how we have used a website or app in the past and use these memories to suggest things that might be of interest to us. This could include people or pages on social media platforms, or even ads for goods and services we might be interested in.

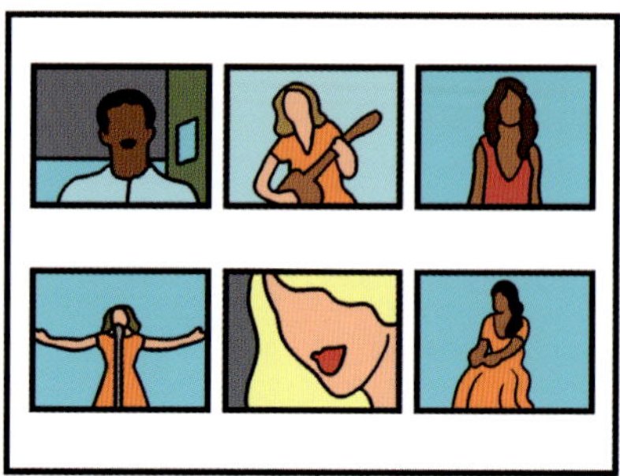

An algorithm can make recommendations for content you can view online based on what you have looked at before and what similar users have also clicked on.

Social media platforms often use algorithms to draw our attention to particular posts based on things we have "liked" or looked at before. For example, when you watch a music video on a platform such as YouTube, an algorithm uses your choice of video to recommend similar songs you might also enjoy.

Algorithms can be helpful and can save us time, but we need to be aware that they can influence our opinions without us realising. Algorithms can also influence our choices about how we spend our time and money.

music videos recommended for you

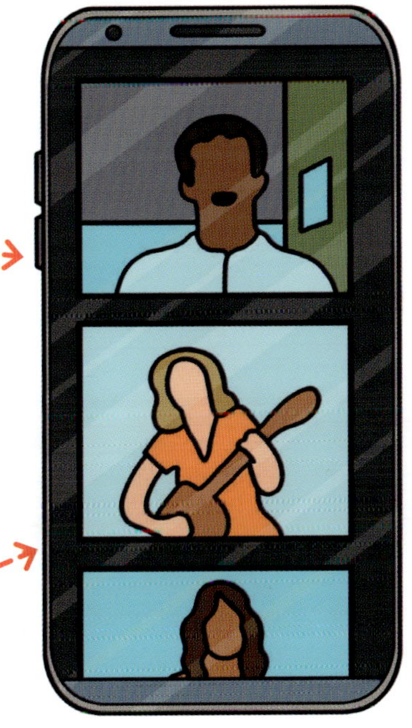

music videos these users watched

Powerful Posts

People who run social media accounts with many followers are known as **influencers**. Influencers usually have a large following related to a particular subject. For example, there are influencers who make regular posts about fashion, travel destinations and restaurants. Some have hundreds of thousands of followers, which gives them power to change people's opinions and even affect their decisions about how and where they spend their money.

Successful influencers can make a full-time living from their work, as they are paid large fees for every photo or video they post. Often, these posts advertise particular products. Influencers are then paid by advertisers who hope an influencer's wide appeal will encourage people to buy the product.

Katherine Sabbath gained half a million followers on social media for her unique cake designs and recipes.

Some people become influencers because they are already successful in a particular field, so their opinions are trusted. Other influencers are initially unknown but develop their online audience through the appeal of their posts.

Mari Copeny

One of the world's most successful young influencers is Mari Copeny, also known as Little Miss Flint. Mari takes her online name from her hometown of Flint, Michigan in the USA, where she has been working to help the Flint water crisis. In September 2022, Mari had around 150 000 followers on Instagram and almost 146 000 followers on Twitter. Mari uses her large following to draw attention to social issues such as protecting the environment, racism and poverty. She won the Changemaker Award at the Billboard Music Awards in 2022 for her work.

Technology such as the internet and headsets allows video game players to connect with other players.

Online Gaming

In the early days of computer gaming, people usually played games alone or next to another person, both using the same screen. The internet, however, has made it possible to play games with multiple players, who can be almost anywhere around the world.

Although people can easily spend too much time playing online games, there are many positives to this kind of gaming. Online games can help young people gain new skills and knowledge, make friends around the world and develop collaboration skills. Some online games are even beneficial for education, for example, games where players work together to design cities or solve environmental problems.

Minecraft

Minecraft is an extremely popular online multiplayer game that was released in 2011. About 140 million players join in every month, working alone or with friends to mine materials and build three-dimensional structures. *Minecraft* can even be used by teachers to help students learn scientific subjects such as chemistry and computer science.

Problematic Programs

Most computer programs are designed to make our lives easier or more enjoyable. Some programs, however, are designed to cause damage to a computer or a network of computers. These **malicious** programs are known as malware. There are many types of malware. Some of the best-known are viruses, which can stop a computer from working properly or damage the files stored in its memory. Another well-known type of malware is spyware. Spyware can secretly monitor what we do on our computers or smart devices, and collect personal data such as passwords and banking information.

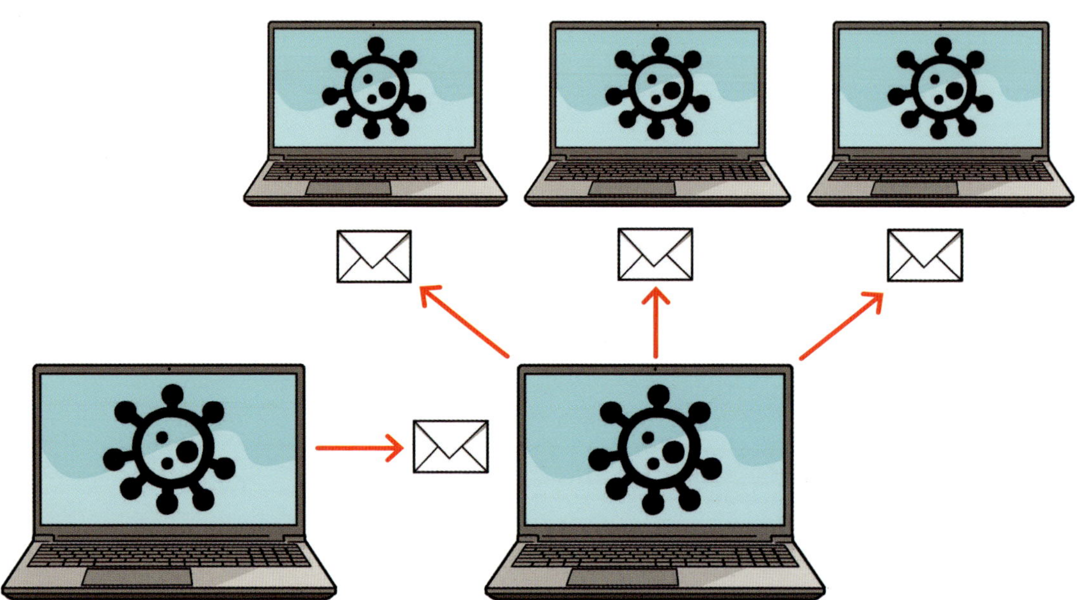

A virus can spread from a hacker's computer to one person through an email, and then be passed on to multiple computers in the same network.

In recent years, ransomware has become another common type of malware. Ransomware is able to digitally lock up a computer so that it can't be used. The ransomware sends a message to the computer's owner, threatening to erase all the files on the computer unless they pay a "ransom", or a specified amount of money.

There are a number of things we can do to prevent ourselves from becoming victims of malware. The most important of these is to install antivirus software, and to be very careful about the kinds of files we open on our devices, especially attachments to emails, as they could contain malware. We also need to be sure that we only download files or software from websites that we know can be trusted.

Hackers have many tools they can use to uncover computer passwords, especially if those passwords are simple.

Accessing Other People's Computers

For as long as the internet has existed, people have used computers to access systems or networks belonging to other people and organisations without permission. This practice is known as hacking. Many hackers have the skills and knowledge to find out passwords so they can access networks containing sensitive information that is intended to be kept private.

Some people use hacking for **political** reasons, for example, to shut down websites of organisations whose views they disagree with. Other hackers use their skills for financial gain by hacking into people's bank accounts to steal their money or using someone's credit card details to make **unauthorised** purchases. Some malicious hackers have even found ways to hack into government computer systems and disrupt important public services, such as healthcare.

Anyone can be a victim of hacking.

Cybersecurity

Cybersecurity is a field of work that has become increasingly important as computers and other internet-connected devices have taken on a larger role in our lives. People who work in cybersecurity strive to counter the effects of malware and prevent computer networks in all sorts of organisations from being hacked.

Before computers were common, most businesses kept important documents and financial information on paper, stored in cabinets. Now, important information is usually stored on computers, and increasingly in internet-based storage systems, which can potentially make the information easier for hackers to access.

Most institutions do almost all their work on computers, which makes cybersecurity very important.

Cybersecurity has become an essential part of business for many institutions, such as schools, banks and hospitals, which are constantly dealing with personal information that needs to be kept private. Being cyber secure is also vital for businesses that need their computer systems to function properly so they can ensure that the supply of goods or services to their customers is not interrupted.

Doctors and nurses often record patient details on internet-connected devices.

The Future of the Internet

Over the coming decades, the internet will continue to grow and change, as will the ways we use it. As it evolves, the internet will become an even greater part of our lives, in ways we can barely imagine today. Our work and study lives will increasingly take place online. For example, for more and more people, it will no longer be necessary to attend school or work in person.

Virtual classrooms allow students and teachers to attend lessons, even from far away.

Many technology experts believe our use of the internet will become less linked to devices such as phones and computers. Although we can already work or attend lessons online, in the future we will be able to "meet" in **virtual** classrooms or workplaces, seeing and interacting with each other as if we were in the same room.

We could do this by using special headsets, or through implants in our ears, eyes or even inside our brains!

A Virtual Excursion

The internet can make all sorts of exciting learning experiences possible. For example, a class in Australia could meet online and enjoy an ultra-realistic three-dimensional excursion to a Tanzanian wildlife reserve together, all without having to leave the safety of home, or risk being attacked by a real lion!

Virtual reality headsets can allow students to experience new ways of learning.

Digital technologies will be part of our lives for a very long time. We will need to keep finding new ways to ensure we can engage with digital technologies safely, and in ways that preserve our privacy. We will also no doubt find many new, positive and exciting ways to enrich our lives with these extremely powerful technologies.

New digital technologies will help us explore the world in ways we can't imagine.

Let's Stay Cyber Safe

A Presentation by Marco

"Cyber safety" is the safe and responsible use of digital communication technologies and devices. Most of us spend many hours online each week, so it's extremely important that we learn about cyber safety and put it into practice as a regular part of our online lives.

Practising cyber safety helps us to avoid online situations where our privacy, self-esteem or even our bank accounts could be put at risk.

The hours we spend online add up quickly, from researching at school to using social media on our phones at home.

Today, students of all ages spend hours every week on screen-based devices, doing homework, playing games, communicating with friends and engaging with social media posts.

Playing online games is a great way to connect with friends.

Because we're all so involved in the online world, we need to take action to stay cyber safe, particularly to prevent breaches of our privacy, such as strangers accessing photos or other personal information on our devices.

Staying Safe on Social Media

Social media presents a wide range of cyber safety issues, particularly when it comes to privacy. When using social media, it's extremely important that we only accept friend requests from people we know in real life, and confirm that the request really came from them.

We also need to know when and where it is safe to use social media. For example, it's always best to use social media under adult supervision, because adults are in a better position to determine if the people we are interacting with are really who we think they are.

An adult can help guide our choices on social media so that we stay safe.

We need to be extremely careful about sharing photos and personal information with strangers on social media, as well as any information about our location. We can unknowingly share this information if we don't change the settings on our devices to prevent this from happening.

Some apps on our devices can track our location without us knowing.

As well as keeping ourselves cyber safe on social media, we owe it to our friends to keep them safe, too. To protect their privacy, it's essential that we ask their permission before posting photos or sharing information about them online.

Posting photos of friends online can be fun, but it's important to make sure everyone in the photo knows what you are posting.

Furthermore, when using social media or playing online games, we can easily find ourselves interacting with people we don't know. For our own safety and privacy, it's very important that we don't share any personal information with anyone whose identity we cannot confirm.

We need to be careful about the information we share with people we can't see online.

Online articles can easily look believable, even if they are not true.

As well as taking care on social media, we need to think carefully about the information we find there. Information presented in articles or videos is not always trustworthy. We need to check who wrote or produced these posts, and consider their reasons for doing so. Sometimes people use their social media accounts to share articles or videos without asking these questions. This can be particularly dangerous when people share medical advice that isn't based on science, or information that could encourage people to make choices that could harm the environment or their health.

There's also a risk that social media can expose us to the awful trauma of cyberbullying. Cyberbullying can take the form of unpleasant private messages, unwelcome sharing of private information or negative comments on social media posts. By carefully monitoring who we interact with, we can reduce the risk of being exposed to this kind of hurtful behaviour.

When we post content online, we can make sure only the people we want to see it have access.

Staying Safe from Malware

Another reason we need to be mindful of cyber safety is that hackers and developers of malware are constantly finding new ways to attack our computers and devices.

To prevent these kinds of damaging attacks, it's vital that we keep the software on our computers or smart devices up to date, particularly the **operating system**.

Hackers are always trying to develop new tools to break through antivirus software.

As hackers find ways to exploit the weaknesses in all kinds of software, software developers are continually producing new versions to address these weaknesses. It's extremely important to check that our devices are running the most recent versions of the apps and software we use, as well as antivirus software, which can stop these malicious attacks.

Finding the Right Balance

It's easy to spend too much time online on our devices, particularly while gaming. As fun and informative as online interactions can be, they can take away precious time from real-world activities such as schoolwork, sports or seeing our friends in person.

It's important to balance our online interactions with spending time with friends in real life.

We now have the opportunity to develop the skills we need to push technology forward in all sorts of exciting directions, but we need to consider how we can do this safely. For example, we can learn **coding** skills to make safe and secure websites, apps and games.

More than anything, our ability to stay cyber safe depends on making good choices every time we go online.

Glossary

algorithm a set of digital instructions that directs a computer to do something, such as sorting social media posts by their likely level of interest to the user

apps applications, or programs, that are downloaded to a mobile device

blogs online collections of a person's writing or videos which are updated regularly, like a public diary

coding the process of writing programs for computers or other digital devices

cyberbullying using messages online to upset someone

hacking getting access to a computer or network without permission

influencers people with many online followers, who recommend different items to buy

malicious intended to do harm

malware software that is meant to cause damage to a computer or network

misinformation false information that is spread to deceive people

operating system the main software that controls how a computer or device functions and allows it to run programs

platforms	online places to post different kinds of content
political	relating to ideas about how a society should operate or how it should be governed
social media	websites that allow users to create and share content with other users
unauthorised	without permission
virtual	not physically present but appearing real through the use of computer programs
viruses	pieces of code in a computer that can spread and cause damage

Index